Two Moms Are Better Than One

BY:

K.C. ECKELS

Library of Congress Control Number: 2015912318

CreateSpace Independent Publishing Platform, North Charleston, SC.

ISBN-13: 978-1515197058

ISBN-10: 1515197050

Printed in the United States of America

TEXT DESIGN BY K.C ECKELS
COVER DESIGN BY K.C. ECKELS
ARTWORK BY K.C. ECKELS

First Paperback Edition

This is for everyone who won the fight for marriage equality

My name is Charlie,

I have a story to share,

I have two moms,

They are the best anywhere.

When people are mean,

That makes me sad,

They don't understand,

The family I have!

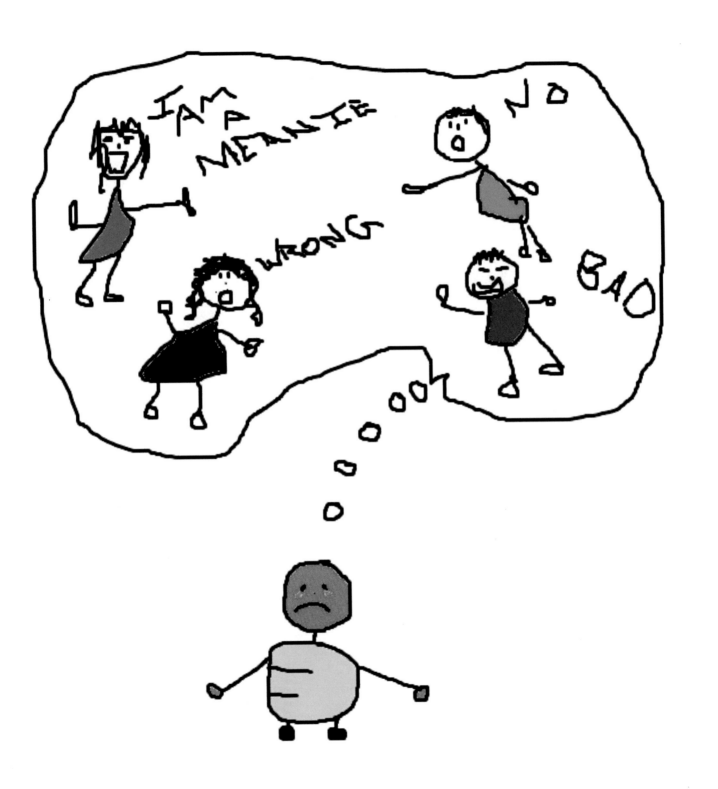

You can see for yourself,

That my family is great!

We go to the park,

And have lots of play dates!

On my first day of school,
I was really scared,
But my Mommies made it better,
By just being there!

For my birthday this year,
I had a party with friends!
I got a lot of great gifts,
But the best one was Fred!
(He's a hamster)

My Mommies got married,
It was a very special day,
I held the rings,
And stayed up real late!

My Moms are the best,

It really is true!

Just last week,

We went to the zoo!

We saw a monkey,
Just hanging around,
While on a train ride,
That went underground!

In the summer my Mommies,

Take me to the pool,

We splash and we swim,

So we can stay cool.

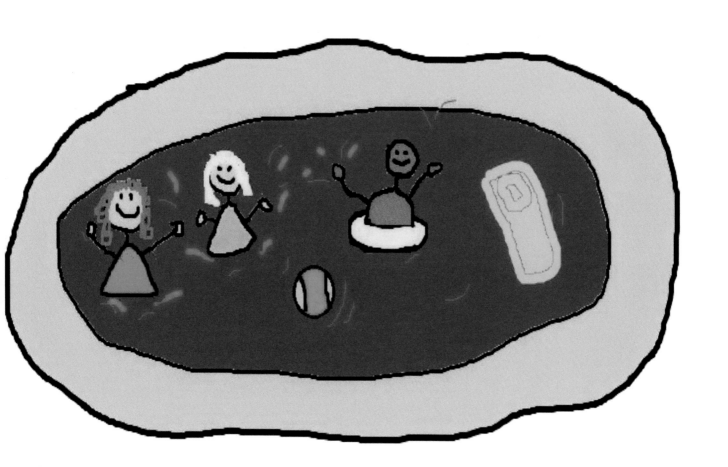

They let me play dress up,
Sometimes they play too,
I pretend we are robots,
That beep and say boo!

We have family dinners,
At six every day,
We sit at the table,
Give thanks and pray.

FAMILY

Sometimes after dinner,
My Moms give me a treat!
Ice cream and cookies,
For dessert is neat!

After we eat,

I have to do chores,

I clean Fred's cage,

And put clothes in my drawers.

Right before sleep time,
I lay in my bed,
My Moms read me stories,
And then kiss my head.

STORY TIME

Having two Moms,
Is so much fun!
I would not want to know,
What it's like to have only one!

All families are different,
But yet still the same,
And if you judge someone,
That's just a shame.

This is my story,
And I'm happy to share,
My wonderful family,
With everyone, everywhere.

MY FAMILY

HER FAMILY

THEIR FAMILY

YOUR FAMILY

Made in the USA
Middletown, DE
10 September 2018